To Macy, Ella, & Sophia,

Ty says Hi!

Little Ty Cooney and the Big Yosemite Race

By Steven Riley

PJS Publishing

For Julie,
Mom, and Dad
Thanks for everything

For further information, contact us at:
PJS Publishing
PO Box 981
Yosemite, CA 95389
pjsrileyss@earthlink.net or pjsriley@yahoo.com

Printed in Hong Kong

Steven Riley
Little Ty Cooney and the Big Yosemite Race

1. Author 2. Title 3.Children's Book
Library of Congress Control Number 2003108907
ISBN 0-9743177-0-5

Little Ty Cooney and the Big Yosemite Race

RUN TY RUN!

There was a day
In the month of May
When the Yosemite animals raced.
El Capitan
Is where it began,
And they all lined up
Before they ran
To make sure their shoes were laced.

The morning was bright.
T'was a beautiful sight
To watch the sun come up.
Tension was high,
The clouds drifted by,
While all of the runners warmed up.

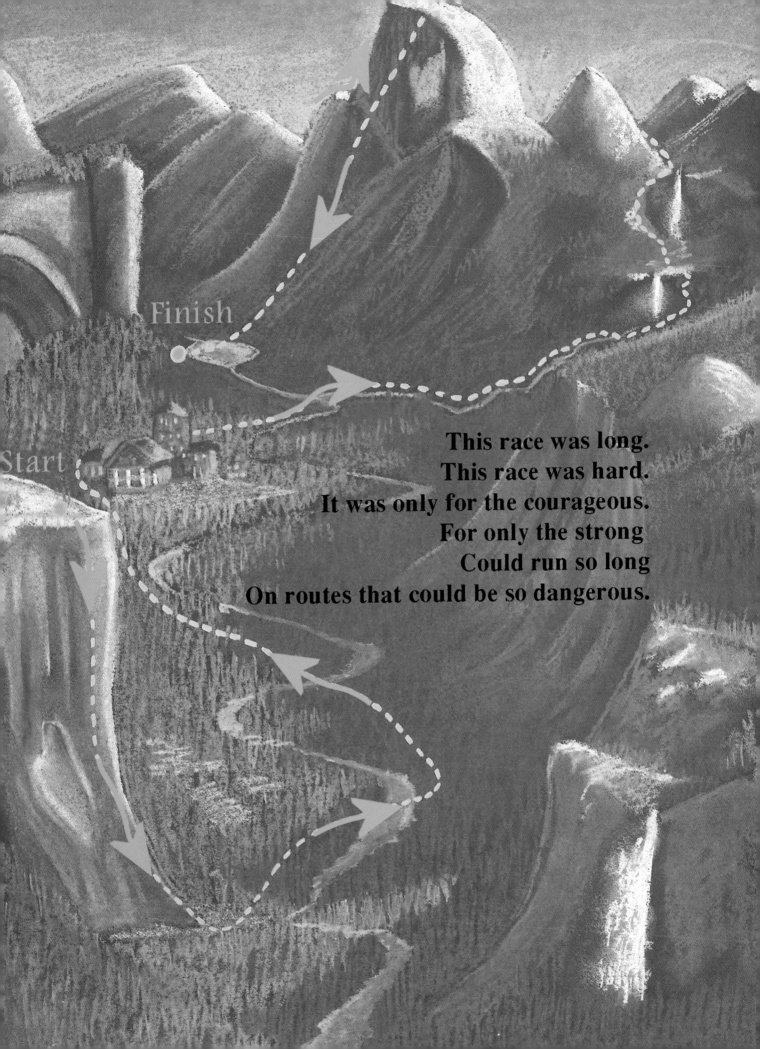

Finish

Start

This race was long.
This race was hard.
It was only for the courageous.
For only the strong
Could run so long
On routes that could be so dangerous.

Yet upon this day
Raced one so young
The others thought he was looney.
No chance did they give
That he'd finish or live,
And this brave young lad's name was Ty Cooney.

But he was determined, this little raccoon,
To overcome this circumstance.
In his heart he knew,
As the start whistle blew,
That he'd have a fighting chance.

For he had practiced
Long and hard,
And time and time again.
'Til he could run this route
Without even a doubt,
And he could run it like the wind.

There was a morning glow
On the valley below
As Ty mounted his goat.
They started the race
Down the Captain's face
While Ty held on to its throat.

He made it down fast
And he wasn't the last,
But there were some others ahead.
He was sure there were four
And quite possibly more,
So he sprinted on toward the Merced.

He jumped in the river~
"Man, is it cold!" He thought
As he fought its flow.
It came from the hills
Where the great water fills
All the falls with the spring's melting snow.

He jumped from the river
And passed Mr. Bear,
Who was caught completely off guard.
You could see the surprise
In his big yellow eyes
As he was passed like a bucket of lard.

Ahwahnee lunch sounded good
As it probably would,
But he knew he'd have to forget it.
For with others to beat
There was no time to eat-
If he stopped, Ty knew he'd regret it.

HAPPY
ISLES
→

Suddenly Ty felt the need
For some serious speed,
And he began to snarl and sneer.
He was haulin' real tail
As he burned up the trail,
And kicked it into high gear.

Then just like that
He passed the bobcat
As they turned up the John Muir Trail
Ty just couldn't miss
For with all his practice
He was sure he wouldn't fail.

Then by Vernal Falls
He passed Mr. Squirrel
Who was looking so thin and frail,
As he panted and swayed
In the water that sprayed
From the falls along the Mist Trail.

To his right was Nevada
With its tall dark cliffs,
And its water that
Thundered and fell.
Then a smile from inside
Crossed his lips
From the pride
That one feels when
One's doing so well.

He could feel his heart beat
Right down to his feet.
He wondered how long he would last.
Then on ahead
Toward the lion he sped,
He was tired, but still running fast.

"I'll win! I'll win!"
He thought
With a grin.
As a redwood watched
Him go.
So he picked up the pace
At the end of the race
While the lion was
Starting to slow.

Then because of the lion's
Refusal to train
He just couldn't take
Any more pain.
So among Half Dome's
Many switchbacks
The lion stopped and
Collapsed in his tracks.
Then with a burst
Of magnificent speed
Little Ty Cooney took
Control of the lead.

Then Ty had to stop
Right there at the top
Of Half Dome to find a way down.
He found a great bird-
Though it does sound absurd
They flew off the cliff toward the ground.

Ty was feeling so fine
As he crossed over the line,
And a smile broke forth from within.
Though Ty was so small
He'd just beat them all,
And that's why this book's
Named after him.

So ended that day
In the month of May
The big race was
Over and done.
It was a big day
For raccoons.
They set free
Their balloons,
For little Ty Cooney
Had...

WON!

THE END

How to draw Ty

You should draw with a pencil so you can erase.

Step 1.
Draw a circle.

Step 2.
Draw the sides of Ty's head and his ears. Erase the circle.

Step 3.
Draw Ty's eyes and nose.

Step 4.
Draw the curved line above Ty's nose. Then draw his mask, and his smile.

Way to go!

How to draw a tree by the Merced

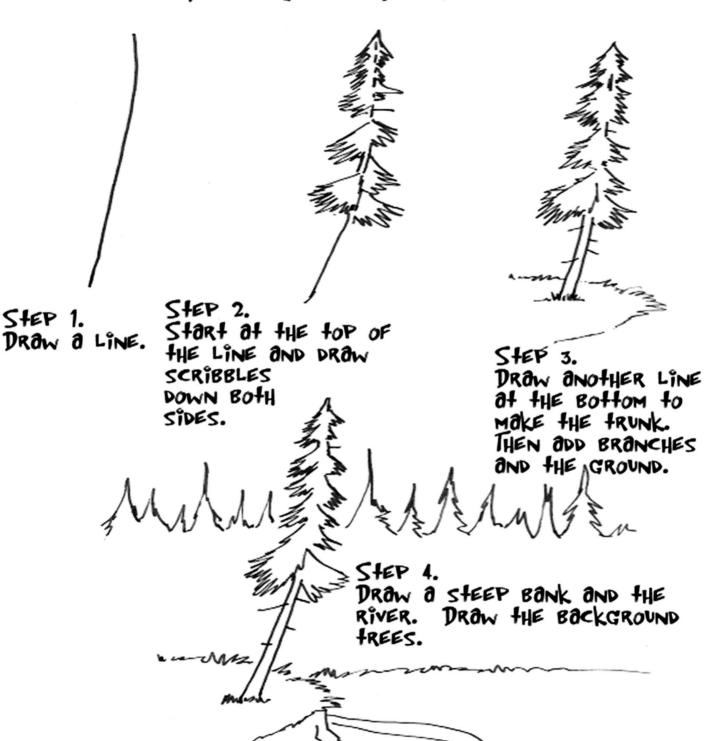

Step 1.
Draw a line.

Step 2.
Start at the top of the line and draw scribbles down both sides.

Step 3.
Draw another line at the bottom to make the trunk. Then add branches and the ground.

Step 4.
Draw a steep bank and the river. Draw the background trees.

You're doing great!

How to draw Half Dome

Step 1.
Draw a square.

Step 2.
Draw a line down the middle of the square, then put the point of Half Dome to the left of the line.

Step 3.
Erase the square and the line. Then draw the top and sides of Half Dome.

Step 4.
Draw the watermarks down Half Dome's face. Then draw the background mountains on both sides.

You're sooo good!

Put it all together.

Now you can draw a picture of Half Dome, the Merced River, and Ty Cooney all together!